Bird House

BLANCA GÓMEZ

ABRAMS BOOKS FOR YOUNG READERS
NEW YORK

En memoria de *la Antonieta*

The illustrations in this book were made with paper collage and digitally.

Cataloging-in-Publication Data has been applied for and may be obtained
from the Library of Congress.

ISBN 978-1-4197-4408-2

Text and illustrations copyright © 2021 Blanca Gómez
Book design by Pamela Notarantonio and Hana Anouk Nakamura

Printed and bound in China
10 9 8 7 6 5 4 3 2 1

Abrams Books for Young Readers are available at special discounts when purchased in quantity for
premiums and promotions as well as fundraising or educational use. Special editions can also be created
to specification. For details, contact specialsales@abramsbooks.com or the address below.

Abrams® is a registered trademark of Harry N. Abrams, Inc.

ABRAMS The Art of Books
195 Broadway, New York, NY 10007
abramsbooks.com

On a snowy day,
my abuela and I found an injured bird.

We brought it home,
and Abuela took care of it.

While the bird was getting better,
my abuela would open its cage
so it could fly around the living room.

It was fantastic.

But everything was always fantastic
at Abuela's house.

When the bird was all better,
my abuela released it from the cage.

"You are cured now, little bird, you have to fly free."

The bird started flying over the city rooftops . . .

. . . until it got lost in the clouds.

Snow melted into spring.

My abuela was watering the plants
when she saw it coming.

"It seems we have a special guest," she said.

"Abuela, can we keep it?"

"No, darling, the bird doesn't belong to us."

"But it can visit anytime."